BOOK CLUB EDITION

HAND, HAND, FINGERS, THUMB

BY AL PERKINS

ILLUSTRATED BY ERIC GURNEY

A Bright & Early Book

RANDOM HOUSE/NEW YORK

 Published in the United States by Beginner Books, a division of Random House, Inc., New York, and simultaneously in Canada by Random House of Canada Limited, Toronto. Library of Congress Catalog Card Number: 76-77841. Manufactured in the United States of America.

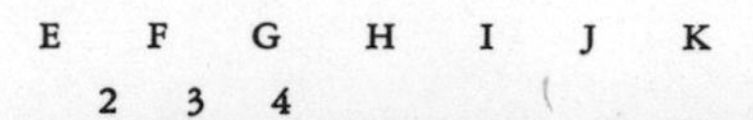
E F G H I J K
2 3 4

Hand
Hand
Fingers
Thumb

One thumb
One thumb
Drumming on a drum.

One hand
Two hands
Drumming on a drum.

Dum ditty
Dum ditty
Dum dum dum.

Rings on fingers.

Rings on thumb.

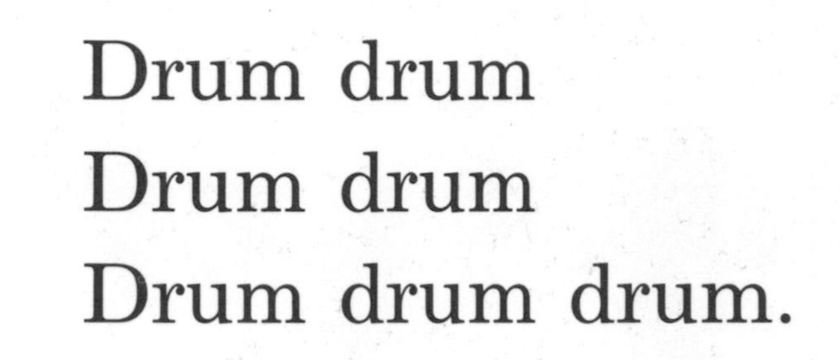

Drum drum
Drum drum
Drum drum drum.

Monkeys drum . . .

. . . and monkeys hum.

Hum drum
Hum drum
Hum drum hum.

Hand picks an apple.

Hand picks a plum.

Dum ditty
Dum ditty
Dum dum dum.

Monkeys come
And monkeys go.

Hands with handkerchiefs.
Blow! Blow! Blow!

"Hello Jack."

"Hello Jake."

Shake hands
Shake hands
Shake! Shake! Shake!

"Bye-bye Jake."

"Bye-bye Jack."

Dum ditty
Dum ditty

Whack! Whack! Whack!

Hands play banjos
Strum strum strum.

Hands play fiddles
Zum zum zum.

Dum ditty
Dum ditty
Dum dum dum,

Hand in hand
More monkeys come.

Many more fingers.
Many more thumbs.
Many more monkeys.
Many more drums.

Millions of fingers!
Millions of thumbs!
Millions of monkeys
Drumming on drums!

Dum
ditty
Dum
ditty
Dum
dum
dum.